GRAFFITI

MIDNIGHT GRAFFITI

J. FALLENSTEIN

darbycreek
MINNEAPOLIS

Darby Creek
A division of Lerner Publishing Group, Inc.
241 First Avenue North
Minneapolis, MN 55401 USA

For reading levels and more information, look up this title at
www.lernerbooks.com.

Images in this book used with the permission of: © A_Lesik/Shutterstock.com (letter graffiti); © Pabkov/Shutterstock.com (heart); © xdrew/Shutterstock.com (spray paint graffiti); © Jaromir Chalabala/Shutterstock.com (alley); © iStockphoto.com/AnnaElizabethPhotography (silhouette); backgrounds: © iStockphoto.com/AF-studio, © iStockphoto.com/blackred, © iStockphoto.com/Adam Smigielski.

Main body text set in Janson Text LT Std 12/17.5.
Typeface provided by Adobe Systems.

Library of Congress Cataloging-in-Publication Data

Names: Fallenstein, J., author.
Title: Graffiti / J. Fallenstein.
Description: Minneapolis : Darby Creek, [2017] | Series: Midnight | Summary: As Lucia Klug tries to make peace with a local bridge where her father died in a truck accident, couples are being harrassed on the bridge and a ghost may be responsible.
Identifiers: LCCN 2016023646 (print) | LCCN 2016037895 (ebook) | ISBN 9781512427677 (lb : alk. paper) | ISBN 9781512430974 (pb : alk. paper) | ISBN 9781512427875 (eb pdf)
Subjects: | CYAC: Bridges—Fiction. | Grief—Fiction. | Dating (Social customs)—Fiction. | Ghosts—Fiction. | Haunted places—Fiction. | Horror stories.
Classification: LCC PZ7.1.F353 Gr 2017 (print) | LCC PZ7.1.F353 (ebook) | DDC [Fic]—dc23

LC record available at https://lccn.loc.gov/2016023646

Manufactured in the United States of America
1-41492-23353-8/16/2016

To Carla Ruth Ahlquist Ketter Heldt, who told me the story of the woman with the long, long fingernails who could scratch her way through solid wood doors was true

CHAPTER 1

SUNDAY

I stare out into the mist from my place in the old rocker on the porch of the duplex, rubbing my thumb and pointer finger over the eagle pendant on the chain at my neck. Just across the highway, the brick frame of the old railroad bridge looks kind of artsy against the white, overcast sky. I should know: I've been staring at it for two weeks now, ever since Mom and I moved here to Middleton. Middle-of-Nowhereton is more like it.

The thing is, I hate bridges. When your dad is driving his truck across a freeway bridge and it collapses below him, you tend to not trust them. And now there's one right in my front yard. Good thing it's shut down. I let the eagle pendant, the only real thing I have left of Dad, drop to my chest.

He's been gone for almost a year now, and I've done everything I can to try and move on. But to be honest, I think I'm getting more and more nervous—more obsessive—as the time passes. Everything at home reminded me and my mom of Dad: our house, the front garden that he landscaped so perfectly, and, worst of all, the construction of the new bridge. Needless to say, we needed a change, so two weeks ago, Mom transferred airline hubs and here we are. Aunt Jane owns this duplex, so now it's Mom and me on one side and Aunt Jane on the other. Kasey, my cousin, also moved in with our aunt a few years ago, after her mom died and her dad kind of checked out of being a parent. Then Kasey's friend Patricia moved in too. Kasey told me Patricia got kicked out of her house and had no place to go, so it was nice of Aunt Jane to take her in as well.

I rock back and forth and sip my chai. Even though I only saw Kasey two or three times a year before we moved here, we have a lot in common. Given everything she's been through, Kasey is one of the few people who, when she says to me, "I know how you feel," really does understand.

Unlike, say, my old school counselor, who categorized me as "lacking emotional wholeness" in the file I probably wasn't supposed to read. Or as "obsessive," though that may be somewhat true because after Dad's accident all I drew or wrote about was bridges. So I know that the bridge in my front yard, for instance, is an old-fashioned arch bridge constructed primarily from large, square bricks. There are iron rails on the top for the safety of pedestrians as well as three massive arches. The bridge that killed Dad was an eight-lane steel-truss arch bridge. Of course, there aren't many people who want to talk for more than, oh, a nanosecond about bridges, so I tend to keep that information to myself.

Now that I live here, it's too bad Kasey is so focused on working and saving money so she can start taking business classes. She went to summer school and got her GED, and now she works at the coffee shop in the mornings and delivers pizzas at night. So at Middleton High I'm Lucia Klug, Six-Foot-Tall Friendless Freak. (I'm actually only five-eleven and three-quarters, but people tend to round up.)

I would hang out with Patricia at school, but she and her boyfriend, Tony, are practically inseparable. Anyway, Patricia's nice enough, but she and connected-at-the-hip Tony are both seniors, two grades above me, and have their own group of friends.

"Lucia!" Mom calls from inside the duplex.

I pull myself out of the rocking chair and go inside.

"I'm doing a three-day to Tokyo. I'll be back Thursday." She's got her flight-attendant suit on. She wipes down the counter, the fridge, and then the sink before adding, "Aunt Jane will be back from her trip tomorrow night. You'll be okay alone? You can see if Kasey will be around tonight."

"Yes, Mom," I say and give her a hug. "Be safe up in that metal tube hurtling through the air."

From the porch I watch her drive past the old railroad bridge. Fighting the urge to shiver, I sit back down in the rocking chair. A cool fall breeze blusters across the porch, and dark clouds hover at the horizon. There will be a storm, but the plane will still take off. The most harmful thing to a plane in the sky is not rain or lightning—it's flocks of birds that get sucked into the engine upon takeoff, disabling the plane and sometimes forcing the pilot to make an emergency landing . . . or worse. Close to five hundred planes have hit bird flocks over my lifetime—or at least since I stopped checking this month, when I made a deal with Kasey that she would get me a job at the Pizza Pit if I stopped researching every fact I came across.

Though the thought of making pizzas doesn't exactly thrill me, having a job would be nice, especially if it was with Kasey. Then we could hang out more, and I'd have spending money, as well as something to do when Mom's flying. I might even make some new friends. Tonight Kasey's early shift should end at eight, and hopefully she will bring home a mistake pizza.

Something sweet wafts out of the open window on the other side of the duplex. I peer in and see Kasey flip her long, black ponytail before taking a cherry pie out of the oven. When she stands up again, I wave at her and walk inside.

"Hey, Lu!" she says with a smile. "Just doing a little baking before my shift. It's the late one tonight."

Working the late shift means she won't be home until after midnight. I'll be home alone again. *Dang.* "Okay," I say, trying not to sound disappointed.

"You all right?" she asks.

I nod, but it feels like there is a five-hundred-pound elephant sitting on my chest.

"Missing your dad?" she asks. "Obsessing?"

"No. Yes. Okay, looking at that weird bridge makes me think of Dad. I keep thinking that if only there was something I could have done—"

"Hey." Kasey points her finger at me. "There is no use going there. I know because

I've done it a million times. What if I'd insisted that Mom go to the doctor the first time she told me she was having heartburn? Maybe then they would have caught the cancer earlier. But you know what? It is what it is—nothing will change it—and we just have to stop with the what-ifs. Besides, we can't waste our energy looking back; we've got a coffee shop to plan!" She steps back, gesturing to the pie on the counter. "And we are going to serve some awesome pies."

I laugh, glad that we're done talking about this heavy stuff. "Where's Drew?" I ask, just now noticing that he's not here.

She shrugs. "Somewhere. I'm not worried about him."

"You don't keep track of his every movement?" I feign surprise.

She smiles. "He's not going anywhere. I've got him hook, line, and sinker." Looking over my shoulder, she says, "Speaking of boyfriends." She frowns and motions to the drive. "Here comes Creepy now."

We watch through the front window as Tony's green truck rumbles up. Patricia is in

the front seat, laughing. Then he and Patricia
kiss for practically eternity, like they don't even
see us standing here, until Patricia finally
gets out.

"Hey, what's up?" Patricia says as she walks
through the front door.

"Hey," I reply.

Tony waves from the truck, but Patricia
doesn't see him so he beeps and waves again.

"Bye!" Patricia blows him a kiss and smiles
as if she's just won the lottery. I take a sip of my
now-cold chai. Tony revs the engine and backs
out, making loose gravel fly.

"What's his rush?" I say.

Patricia shrugs and says, "He's just a
goofball," then vanishes into her bedroom.

Tony fishtails as he zooms past the old
bridge. He's so reckless, even when he's so
close to that bridge. Something about it gives
me the creeps.

I need to get over this fear because I can't
live always afraid of bridges—how will I get
anywhere? Like, literally? I'm certainly not
staying here in Middle-of-Nowhereton forever.

I'm moving with Kasey to Portland or Seattle to start that coffee shop right after I graduate.

I set my empty cup on the porch ledge and walk down the old road, stopping at the bank of the river. The bridge looms a few feet ahead. Tall grass and weeds have grown over the train tracks, and new three-foot-tall wood barriers stand on both ends of the bridge. There must have been an accident recently.

Still, it's not reasonable to be afraid of bridges—of this bridge. There's no construction equipment, like there had been on Dad's bridge; heck, there aren't ever any cars or trains on it either. I step up to the bridge and lift my leg over the barrier.

CHAPTER 2

SUNDAY

The bridge looks at least a hundred years old, probably more. Does the Department of Transportation even inspect unused bridges? I wonder. I probably should have checked that before climbing out onto the crumbling old death trap. But I want to walk across it. I want to conquer my fear. I stand at the edge of the bridge. The wood planks of the tracks and the bricks beneath them appear solid. And the iron handrails seem sturdy. But, as always, my radar is up and running, looking for faults.

The river rushes below, green and frothing and murky, but not as deep as the mighty

Mississippi, the river Dad's bridge collapsed into on that horrible day. I have to remind myself that this is not that river. The periphery of my vision closes in until it's all a blur and little dots appear. I grasp the iron bar with my slick palm and close my eyes.

I can do this, I say to myself. *I can just hurry across and back and then I'll have conquered my fear. Kasey will be so proud of me.*

The tracks run down the middle of the bridge. I take one tentative step on the worn, gray planks, then another.

A bird squawks from its perch in a tree on the river bank. My legs ignore my brain's directions and go limp; I collapse into a squat. "Go away, bird!" I say into my palms.

I practice my box breathing: four counts in, hold for four, four counts out, hold for four. The problem is that I know too much. This railroad bridge could have a design flaw similar to the one that led to Dad's bridge collapse. The bricks could be too old or so worn that they might crumble when too much weight is on the bridge and drop everything above it into the river. When Dad died, the reports said the additional weight of construction vehicles on the bridge "contributed to the collapse, creating a catastrophic failure." *Catastrophic* was right, but why did it have to be Dad? It was my fault after all: I could have asked for a ride home from practice from someone else, and then he wouldn't have been on the bridge when it collapsed.

Lucia, don't go there. Stop thinking about that, I chide myself. Refocusing my attention to *this* bridge, I let out a long breath. *Can I do this?* Almost immediately, my mind circles back to Dad's bridge, with its piers and longitudinal deck stringers and reinforced concrete pavement and transverse expansion joints. I put my hands over my ears. After the collapse the city brought in Navy divers and used sonar to find the submerged cars. The governor showed up, and it took thirteen hours to find the thirteen people who died. One was Dad.

That bridge is gone, just like Dad.

I need to move on because the rest of my life is not in the past, it is ahead of me. I

take a breath and slowly stand. The hazy sky,
riverbanks, and iron supports whirl around me.
A whimper makes its way up my throat, and
tears well up in my eyes.

Not today, bridge, not today.

Carefully I put my hand on the bridge's
iron handrail. Mist rises from the river. If my
legs would just stop shaking I could get back
over the barrier, back to solid land and safety.
A creak sounds behind me and a chill passes
like a cold hand on my neck. I sense something
behind me.

My heart pounds. *It's only the mist,* I remind
myself. I've been on this bridge more than long
enough. My feet stumble on top of each other
as I race back to the edge of the bridge. Before
I know it I'm back to the barrier. I throw
myself over it onto solid ground.

I need to sit somewhere and chill before
I head home. I walk around the barrier and
down the grassy embankment to a large stone
a few feet from the water. The river's not scary
when you're just next to it, on solid land.

The stone is still warm from the sun.

Under the bridge, someone has written something on a faded patch of bricks.

Annie + Alex 2gether 4ever.

How cute. I roll my eyes and lean forward. There are more names.

Isobel & Henry = love is written in red.

And there, to the right, in white spray paint: **Kasey-n-Drew r tru.**

Kasey! I picture her coming here with Drew, spraying their names on the bridge.

My eyes lose focus as I stare at each of the names. I shift my gaze to the river, hoping to steady my vision. All of a sudden the water seems to reflect something—a face. A skull.

I pull my glasses off my face and try to rub the image of the skull out of my eyes. *Wow, I have really freaked myself out this time.*

Above me, someone is climbing over the barrier. I slide my glasses back on.

"Hey!" I call. "Patricia!"

"Lucia?" she says. "What are you doing here?"

"Me?" I say as I scramble up the grassy slope. "Just checking out this cool old bridge."

I try to sound upbeat, like it doesn't scare the color right out of my face.

"Some say it's haunted," Patricia says.

"Haunted?" I keep my voice level.

"By Billy Jones."

"Billy Joel, the singer?"

Patricia sighs. "Funny. Obviously not, as it happened in 1880. His girlfriend dumped him, so he jumped, and now his ghost haunts the bridge."

My slippery hand rests casually on the barrier. "There's an actual ghost?"

Patricia nods.

"You really believe that?" *Should I tell her about the skull?*

"Yeah, people have seen it. Not only that, but Billy also supposedly cursed the place when he jumped. Don't ever come out here at night."

"And here I was planning a midnight picnic." We turn to head back to the house together. "Wait, I thought you were going to work."

"The store was dead, no big coupons this week, so I left a little early and had Tony pick me up."

"Is something wrong with your car?"

"Yeah, but it's just the fuel pump. Tony will fix it; he's good with cars."

Walking alongside her down the road, I think of the names under the bridge. *Annie + Alex 2gether 4ever.* I picture the tall girl with the turquoise hair from my art class, a junior who did a watercolor of a bunch of hearts. "Is Annie still dating Alex?" I ask.

"Yeah," Patricia says. "They say they'll be together forever, even though they've only been together for two months." When we get to the porch she says, "See on you on the flip flop," and goes into her side of the duplex.

It isn't until I am boiling water for another chai that it occurs to me: if the bridge is so creepy and haunted, what was Patricia doing there?

CHAPTER 3

MONDAY

I barely get up in time to walk the six blocks to Middleton High. It's a good thing my first period is working as an assistant for the school counselor, Mrs. Whyse, and I can sleepwalk through my next couple of classes after that.

At lunch, just as I step out of the line with my tray of food, I hear an argument. It's Annie, the turquoise-haired junior from art class. She flips a guy's tray over, and peas and carrots fly everywhere.

"Annie!" the guy says, holding up his hands. "Nothing happened!"

"You said you were just giving her a ride home!" Annie screams. "It doesn't take two hours to drive across town!" The whole lunchroom watches the drama. Annie pulls a silver necklace from around her neck and hurls it at him. "We are done."

I realize I've just been standing around staring when Mrs. Whyse passes me with her own lunch. Together we watch Annie storm off.

"What just happened?" I ask.

"I think Annie and Alex broke up," she says before continuing toward the counseling office.

"2gether 4ever"? I guess not, I think to myself. Wanting more answers, I follow her with my tray. As we leave the cafeteria, I spot Tony and Patricia sitting together out of the corner of my eye. They get up and empty their trays into the big gray garbage tub. I lift my hand to wave to Patricia, but she doesn't seem to notice me. *Figures.* She never notices anything when Tony is around.

A few steps later, we've reached the counseling office, and I try to pry Mrs. Whyse for more information.

"Hey Mrs. Whyse, you've lived here for a while, right?"

"All my life," she says.

"Do you know anything about that old railroad bridge—the Billy Jones story?" I ask.

Mrs. Whyse sets down her lunch and cocks her head. "That old legend?"

"Yeah," I say as I sit down to join her. "How does it go again?"

"It's said that if a couple writes their names on the old bridge at midnight, they will be together forever. Kids were doing it so much that the bridge looked trashy, so they finally sandblasted it clean last summer."

That must mean the names I saw on it were added after that. *But why would Patricia say not to go there at night if writing on the bridge brings couples luck? Where does the curse fit in?* I try not to think about what I saw in the water. "What does that have to do with the curse?"

"Supposedly Billy Jones jumped off the bridge when his girlfriend broke up with him," says Mrs. Whyse. "Some people say that he set the curse as he jumped."

"What does the curse do?"

"They say that any couple who writes
their names on the bridge can never break up.
If they do, Billy Jones will come after them.
Ever since then, local couples have seen it as a
challenge, thinking that their relationship is
worth the risk." She looks like she wants to say
even more.

"Do *you* think it's cursed?"

She shrugs. "Last summer, right after it was
finally cleaned, a couple wrote their names on
the bridge, and then they broke up and . . . "

I lean in. "What? What happened?"

"They were in a car accident. They
somehow went off the road and drove
straight at the bridge—the barrier was
so decayed that they almost went right
through it. The girl, Isobel, said she saw
someone on the bridge who was about to
jump, but when the police came no one
was there."

"Did anyone die?" I almost don't want to
know. Yet I have to know, like how you have to
look at an accident on the highway.

"No. Isobel had a mild concussion and a broken ankle, and Henry had whiplash and a cut on his wrist."

Isobel and Henry, the same names under the bridge!

"But since the accident," Mrs. Whyse continues, "no one really goes near the bridge anymore, except the teenagers who think their love can withstand, despite the curse. And the city installed those new barriers to keep them away."

"So it *is* haunted," I say. "You think so too."

"Every story has two sides. Check the library sometime for the old articles," she says. Her office phone rings. As she gets up to answer it she says over her shoulder, "Decide for yourself."

I try to focus on the rest of my food, but I can't stop thinking about the bridge. I check the clock. There's fifteen minutes left before lunch is over, and my curiosity wins out: I hurry to the library. There's no way I will be able to concentrate on political science without getting to the bottom of this story.

This is the first time I've been to the school library since moving here. It's smallish with shelf-lined walls, three computers, and a single table in the middle.

"May I help you?" asks an older woman in jeans and knee-high black leather boots as she steps out of a tiny back office. She looks at me through round, red-rimmed glasses. Her short hair is gray, and the very tips are dyed purple.

"Yes, I'm looking for some newspaper articles on Billy Jones."

She raises her eyebrows. "Billy Jones? Why?"

"Mrs. Whyse sent me to do research," I say.

Her head tilts. "Mrs. Whyse sent you?"

"Yes," I say loudly and with conviction because, well, it's technically true.

"Well then, wait one moment please."

She disappears back into her office and shuts the door. I hear some shuffling around before she comes out with a large brown folder. "These are copies," she says. "I ordered them at the beginning of the school year when kids started asking about the ghost. Don't take them or write on them or damage them in any way." She sets the folder on the table.

I sit down and eagerly open the folder. It contains a small stack of photocopied pages, the first being the front page of the *Middleton Times* from July 1880. There, among the ads for *Pianos $10* and *Goodyear Rubber* and *Buy the Finest Spectacles $2, $2.5, $3*, is a small paragraph:

Suicide in Middleton. July 3, Billy Jones, about 18 years of age, committed suicide last night about midnight by jumping off the railroad bridge. His body was found drowned in the river to-day near where he went into the water.

I jump when the bell rings. The next period is going to start in a few minutes. "Find what you were looking for?" the librarian asks.

"Nothing about a curse," I say.

"Of course not," she says, taking the folder from my hand. "People never gave it much thought until last year's accident."

***

For the rest of the day, I can't concentrate. The algebra teacher calls on me twice before I hear her. I think about Billy Jones the whole way home. When I walk up the driveway, Kasey is sitting in the rocking chair on the porch in her black Pizza Pit hoodie. "Hey, Lu. What's up?" she asks.

"There was a fight today at school."

Her eyes widen. "At Middleton? No way!"

"Not like a physical fight. It was Annie and Alex. They broke up, I guess. She flipped his lunch tray!"

"Oh." Kasey sounds sad. "They were such a cute couple."

"Maybe they're cursed." I sit on the steps of the porch.

"Cursed? Why?"

"The names-on-the-bridge-at-midnight thing."

"Oh, that," she says.

"I saw your name there."

"Kasey-n-Drew r tru." She laughs. "I wrote that."

"Why did you write your names if the bridge is cursed?"

"If you write your name at midnight, you'll

stay together. I had to do it, Drew was too chicken."

"Really?" I ask. "Was he afraid of getting in trouble or the curse?"

"He's superstitious. The curse thing freaks him out."

"So you're making a promise to each other?"

Kasey shrugs and flips her ponytail. "I don't know. It's just for fun. So Annie and Alex broke up, whatever. They're not the first."

"But what about the Billy Jones curse?"

"Maybe people like a challenge. Nothing says 'I love you' like defacing a cursed bridge, right? Look at what happened to Isobel and Henry—they wrote their names on the bridge, broke up, and then—"

"Yeah, didn't they have an accident near the bridge?"

She nods. "They thought they saw someone about to jump."

"Maybe writing your name on that bridge is just bad luck," I say.

Kasey stands up. "Maybe. But since both my name and Drew's are on it, I hope not.

Sorry, Lu, I've got to get to work." She walks down the steps to her car. "I'll be home at ten. And I'll bring home any mistake pizzas," she promises. "What kind of mistake are you hungry for?"

"Any! But pineapple and ham would be a nice mistake," I say.

"Gross," she says, but then grins. "Just kidding. By the way, I've got some new ideas for our coffee shop. Let's talk about them over pizza when I get home." She waves and gets into her car.

Kasey backs out of the driveway and drives past the bridge. My eyes stop on the gray iron rails.

After writing their names this summer, two couples have already broken up. Apparently graffiti doesn't keep you together. I think about the bridge that night as I'm falling asleep. I have to find out more. And I know where to do it.

CHAPTER 4

TUESDAY

The next morning I put on my glasses and throw my hair into a messy ponytail. My eyes are puffy. I don't usually wear much makeup to school, but this morning I add a thick coat of concealer to the dark bags beneath my eyes.

I woke up at midnight sweating, with the sheets tangled around my legs. I had to turn the light on because the dream I had was so creepy: I walked into an old house that was lit with four candles. Then in one of the rooms it was completely dark and I fell, but it wasn't a regular room—it was a cliff. Then I was underwater and the weeds were grabbing my legs and holding me under.

My lack of sleep concealed, I guzzle a glass of water and scan the fridge for something quick to eat. I grab a cold piece of last night's mistake pizza. It doesn't taste as good as it did then, but that may be because Kasey isn't here to enjoy it with me. Spending time with her was so great—it finally felt like old times.

As I hurry out the door, I pass by the bridge. Despite my nightmare, I'm still in a good mood from last night, so I won't let it get to me today.

I step into the counseling office just after the bell rings. As I settle into my filing work, the phone rings and Mrs. Whyse picks up. "What about Alex?" she says. "Tell me what happened." I quickly sit at my desk and pretend to be busy stapling orientation packets together. "Last night?" she says and glances up at me. "Why was he out riding at midnight?"

I'm not even bothering to pretend to work anymore. She's caught my full attention.

"I see. Is he all right?" Silence again.

Then Mrs. Whyse says, "Yes, of course." She hangs up and makes another call, but this time she gets up and closes her door. I tiptoe over and lean my ear against it.

Mrs. Whyse is practically whispering. "He was riding his bike through the park, and he said a black truck was behind him with its high beams on, trying to run him off the road." After a pause she says, "No, he couldn't see, but he said it was someone in a black hoodie with the hood up. He's pretty shaken up. We don't want any more of these curse rumors spreading—that will cause hysteria." She hangs up and opens the door before I can step away.

"Lucia?" she says, "Did you need something?"

I cough. "A—A loose staple fell, um, under the desk. I can't find it."

"There's a flashlight in the bottom drawer," she says.

I walk back to the desk and crouch down, pretending to use the flashlight to find the staple. Fortunately, Mrs. Whyse isn't even paying attention to me. I start to realize the reality of the situation: Someone—or something—was after Alex. *Is it the ghost of Billy Jones?*

Mrs. Whyse was right about rumors: everyone is talking about Alex by the time first hour lets out. Patricia stops me in the hall and asks if I've heard about how the ghost of Billy Jones chased Alex through the park and tried to kill him.

"Don't tease," I say. "It's scary. And where's Tony? I'm not sure I've ever seen you two apart. You look like half a sandwich without him."

"He's sick, slept late," she says before hurrying up the stairs to talk to a group of older girls about the ghost.

Later, in the middle of lunch, I see Annie run into the cafeteria. Her turquoise hair flies in all directions as she screams and points down the hall.

Hearing the screams from the nearby counseling office, Mrs. Whyse rushes into the lunch room and over to Annie. "Tell me what happened," she says.

"In the bathroom," Annie wails and points down the hall. They run to the girls' bathroom, and I can't help but follow.

I reach the bathroom a few steps behind them. Annie is pacing and trying to collect herself in order to tell the story. "The lights went out," she sobs. "I asked who was there, but no one answered. Finally I came out of the stall and turned the lights on and saw *that* . . ."

LIAR is smeared across the mirror in sticky red . . . something.

Annie breaks down, and Mrs. Whyse wraps an arm around her.

Why would someone write "liar"? This can't be the work of a ghost, can it? In the girls' bathroom? The rest of the day all I can think about is the curse and the bridge. *I have to go back there*, I think. *Maybe there's some clue I missed.*

After my last class I stop at my desk in the counseling office, grab the small flashlight, and head out.

The sky is overcast. I'll have to hurry because I refuse to be stuck near a broken-down bridge during a big thunderstorm. When

I reach the barrier, I set my backpack down and sit for a moment to steady myself. I climb over the barrier and step on the planks as soon as I feel prepared. Raindrops speckle the planks, and the old wood is slippery. I climb back over the barrier. I can't cross now. Not today.

I head down the slope to check the names. A faint black line of spray paint crosses out Isobel's name. Fog drifts over the water. A gust of wind whips through the iron rails and makes a *whoooo* sound, like a long sob. The hairs on my neck stand up.

I run the flashlight's beam back over each set of names. I noticed something I hadn't seen before. I can just make out letters in gold spray paint: C-L-E-O. *This looks unfinished, I think to myself. What if the ghost caught the couple while they were writing it and scared them away?* I lean forward a bit more to see if I can find any more writing, but my foot slips and sinks into thick mud at the river's edge. I lean into the grassy slope, grab a fistful of grass, and try to pull my foot out. But the mud is like quicksand. The harder I pull, the harder it sucks my foot back in. At that moment, the sprinkling turns into a full-on downpour. My jeans are coated up to my calf with mud and my heart starts racing.

I try to get my footing in the slick grass, but it's too slippery. Lightning flashes just as I fall, slipping into the river. I gasp in surprise as icy water comes up to my shoulders and shocks my body. Grass and mud from the fall coat my teeth and catch in my throat, making breathing feel impossible. Completely panicked, I almost give in to the river, but then I see my dad's face.

No, I think, *I'm not ready to die. Not now, not like this.*

Clinging to that thought, I grasp a handful of weeds with my frozen fingers and twist my foot until it comes free.

Drenched, I crawl up the battered slope through the downpour. I grab my backpack and run.

CHAPTER 5

TUESDAY

As I race back to the duplex, a big, dark truck passes me on the road; it kicks up dirt and muck into my wet hair. When I finally get home, I hear arguing coming from Kasey's side of the duplex. I drop my wet backpack on the porch and slink along the house. I crouch behind where Drew's car is parked in the side yard and listen.

"I thought you didn't apply," Kasey says accusingly.

"It's only for five months," Drew pleads. "It's an opportunity of a lifetime."

"But Mexico?" Kasey says. "It might as

well be Mars. I'll never see you! I can't believe you're leaving me all alone here. You said we'd be together. You promised."

"And we will," Drew says. "It's just a few months."

"Remember the curse? Bad things happen to the couples that break up after they've written their names on the bridge. Remember Henry and Isobel's accident last year? And look what just happened to Alex and Annie! We could be next," Kasey says between sniffles.

"That's not fair, Kasey—you know how much the curse freaks me out," Drew snaps. "Can we just talk about this later, when you're not acting crazy?"

"Fine!" Kasey yells. "If you think I'm acting crazy, we might as well just break up. Then we'll see if this curse is real."

It turns out I didn't even need to go to the bridge to search for clues—Kasey has had the answers this whole time. *Couples aren't cursed just for putting their names on the haunted bridge, they're cursed if they've put their names on the bridge and then they break up.* All the pieces are coming together now, but one thing is still bothering me. *I've asked Kasey about the curse before—why didn't she tell me what she knew?*

I'm so lost in my thoughts that I almost don't notice Drew storming out of the duplex, heading toward his car—which I'm still crouched behind. I sprint to the front of the duplex, mud flying off my jeans, hoping it looks like I'm just trying to get out of the rain. But Drew is so upset he doesn't even see me. I hurry up to the window just in time to see Patricia give Kasey a hug. Coming through the front door, I see Kasey wiping away her tears.

"Hey, Lu," she says. "What happened? You look like the swamp monster."

At Kasey's words, my body freezes up again. I try to forget what just happened at the bridge. Instead I turn my attention to the warm air and sweet smell in the kitchen. A pumpkin pie sits cooling on the counter; the buttery nutmeg-and-cinnamon combination makes my mouth water. Patricia lifts a laundry basket. "Gotta change over my laundry," she says. "Sorry about you and Drew."

I try to look surprised. "What's going on?"

Kasey sits at the dining room table. "Drew's breaking up with me for the exchange program." A plate on the table has a small piece of yesterday's cherry pie on it, and she stuffs a forkful into her mouth.

"Did he say he wanted to break up, though?" *Because that's not what it sounded like* . . .

She shakes her head. "It's just five months, but it might as well be a lifetime. If only I was still in school, I could go on the program with him."

I know Kasey is upset, but we have more important topics to discuss—starting with the strange dark truck that raced past me on my way home. "Not to change the subject," I say, deliberately changing the subject, "But do you know anyone who drives a black truck?"

"Lots of people drive trucks here," she says, brushing pie crumbs from her black hoodie. "Drew's uncle has a truck. It's gray, though. He was going to sell it to Drew, but now that Drew is moving to the far reaches of the planet I guess he won't. Too bad, I really like that truck. I drove it last night when I helped Drew move some of his stuff into his uncle's basement."

"You drove it? What time?" I can't help but ask.

"It was after midnight when I finally got home," she says, and she swipes some cherry filling off the plate and into her mouth. Thick, sticky, red goo. Just like on the mirror in the bathroom.

"Are you okay?" Kasey asks, staring at me.

"Oh, yeah. Just thinking. Um, do you have some quarters? I only have bills and I need to go down and do laundry too."

"Sure, Lu."

"Where's Aunt Jane?"

"She was back, but now she's on another work trip." We go into the kitchen, and I dig into my backpack and hand her two bills as she takes a rectangular gold box from the countertop. It looks Egyptian, with a golden woman wearing a bird on her head next to a man with some hieroglyphics underneath. Kasey opens the box and takes out eight quarters.

"Neat box," I say.

"Yeah, it was a gift. Last Christmas . . . " She pauses to hand me the quarters, shakes her head and sniffles, and seems to realize why she was holding the box in the first place. "Hey, do you need soap? I left a big jug down there; go ahead and use some. Now excuse me while I go lie down and cry my eyes out."

Patricia comes into the kitchen through the back door from the basement and motions for me to come closer. "Did Drew really break up with her?" she whispers.

"Sort of?" I whisper back. "I'm not really sure what's going on."

"Wait, they actually broke up?!" Tony's harsh voice suddenly comes out of Patricia's laundry basket. Just now I notice her phone sitting on the pile of clothes—she must have him on speaker. "So much for promising to be together! I thought their love was 'tru' . . . "

Before Tony can continue, Patricia hastily turns off the speaker. "Ugh, anyway," she says, "I have so much laundry to do. It's a drag to pay for it. Should be free if we live here, right?"

"Yeah, but at least you've got a place to stay since you got kicked out."

Patricia narrows her eyes. "I didn't get kicked out."

"You didn't?"

"No," she says, cheeks flushed. Patricia starts to turn away from me, but then adds, "I get along great with my parents. They're remodeling, that's all."

That isn't what Kasey said, I think.

I want to ask her more, but Patricia quickly says, "Hey, I used up the dryer sheets that were down there," she says. She's out of the kitchen before I can even respond. *I guess that conversation's over.*

Needing to grab some dryer sheets from our side of the duplex, I head to the front door and pass Kasey's bedroom. She's lying on her bed, crying into a pile of teddy bears.

CHAPTER 6

WEDNESDAY

"Patricia! Lu! Come look at this!" I hear Kasey yell from the driveway early the next morning.

Kasey stands at her little red car, holding a piece of paper.

"What is it?" I rush down the front steps, with Patricia right behind me, as she holds the paper out. In scratchy letters it reads, "People who brake promises get hurt."

"What does this mean?" Kasey asks.

"It's the curse!" Patricia says.

"Shut up, Patricia!" Kasey snaps, shaking her head. "Besides, Drew's the one who chose Mexico over me! I didn't break anything!"

"Wait," I say. "It says *brake*, like car brakes. What if someone messed with your car? I don't think you should drive it."

"I've got to get to work," Kasey says. "Patricia, can you call Tony? He's good with cars, he can look at them."

"He's already on his way here, but he can't be late anymore or he'll get suspended. Sorry," Patricia says, not sounding sorry at all.

"I guess I'll call Drew," Kasey says, obviously hurt by Patricia's lack of concern. "I can drop him off at school and use his car—if he'll let me."

Just then, Tony's truck pulls up. Without a word, Patricia gets in, and the truck squeals out onto the road. *Jeez*, I think. *She could have at least mentioned Kasey's brake issue to Tony.*

By the time I'm ready for school, Drew pulls up. I sling my backpack over my shoulder and notice he looks less than thrilled about helping Kasey with her car. Watching through the screen door, I can't help but wonder how *this* will turn out.

Kasey winces as Drew slams the car door. "What's wrong with *you*?" she asks, clearly taken aback by his attitude.

Drew reaches in through his open window and pulls out a teddy bear with a knife in it. Both of its eyes are ripped out. He flings it at Kasey's feet. "You think this is funny?"

"Whoa!" Kasey lifts her hands and takes a step back. "What are you talking about?"

Red-faced, Drew shakes his head. "Leaving this on my front steps? Kasey, my *mom* found it. Practically gave her a heart attack."

"Me?" Kasey says, "I didn't do that."

"Then who did?" Drew asks. "The ghost of Billy Jones?"

"Well, it wasn't me," she says, her voice trembling. She grabs the note from her pocket. "Drew, someone left this on my car." He reads the note and his face softens. He wraps her in a tight hug, and they murmur to each other.

I'm going to be late for school if I don't leave now. Kasey and Drew pull apart as I open the door. Kasey wipes her eyes, and Drew slides into her front seat, looking under the dash. He pops the hood and inspects what I assume is the car's braking system.

"I can't tell if anything is wrong," he says, "But you should definitely take the car in to have the brakes looked at. It's not safe to drive until you know for sure."

"Can I borrow your car to get to work?" Kasey asks. "I'll drop you off at school first." Then she turns to me as I come down the porch steps. "Want a ride?" I nod appreciatively and hop in.

On the way to school I ask, "Who do you think did those things?"

Drew shakes his head. "Somebody who's not right in the head."

***

As I three-hole-punch papers for Mrs. Whyse, my thoughts turn back to Kasey and the weird note. It has to be something about the breakup. Who else knew about it besides me and Patricia? It couldn't have been Patricia because I was up until past midnight doing algebra, and I didn't see or hear her leave to go to Kasey's car. A chill comes over me. *It's not a ghost*, I tell myself. *It has to be someone here in Middleton. But who?*

Be logical, Lu, I tell myself. If I were a detective, I'd talk to others who have their names on the bridge, other potential victims. Isobel and Henry graduated, but Annie and Alex are still here. Maybe they could give me a clue as to who's doing these things.

At lunch I plop down next to Annie like we've been friends since preschool.

"Hey," I say. "How's it going?"

She takes a slow bite of her burger. "You're the new girl," she says.

"Yep. We have art together."

She takes another bite and looks around as if maybe she's at the wrong table.

"So," I say, "you and Alex broke up."

"Alex and me? Everybody knows." She flips her hair over her shoulder.

She looks at me like maybe I've got something contagious. I ignore it and continue. "I saw the mirror in the bathroom. It said 'liar.'"

"Oh. Yeah. That was creepy."

"Any idea who did that? Do you think it's about the breakup?"

"I don't know," she says as she chews. "Maybe it was the girl Alex drove home from the party."

"But why would she write 'liar'?" I ask. "You'd think she'd be happy you guys broke up, not sad."

Annie takes a drink of her milk and shakes her head. "You're right, I don't know," she says.

"Did you see who followed you in?"

"Yeah," she says.

"You did?" I sit bolt upright.

"You."

I sink back down, exasperated. "No," I say. "I mean right after you first walked in, before you came out of the stall."

She shakes her head and takes another gulp of milk. "Somebody who doesn't like it when people break up, I guess." Now her look says that I'm the one at the wrong table.

I try not to roll my eyes. *This has been absolutely no help. Time to change tactics.*

"What about Alex? Did he ever see who tried to run him off the road?"

She sighs. "Somebody in a black hoodie. That's all I know. It's probably the curse. The same thing happened to Henry."

"What? What same thing?" I say.

"After Henry and Isobel broke up—a few weeks after the accident, he went to the bridge to get rid of their names and someone, like, came at him in the dark. They struggled for a while, and Henry got hurt pretty bad: crushed fingers. His hand got smashed or stepped on or something, and then he was pushed into the river."

"So what happened to him?"

"I mean, he was fine. Dude is on the swim team. He was freaked out, though—said he got stuck so deep in the mud he almost drowned." I swallow nervously, trying not to think about my own recent incident at the bridge.

"And nobody figured out who crushed his fingers?" I say.

She raises both eyebrows at me, and then her two friends with equally colorful hair sit down and *also* look at me like I'm at the wrong table. Clearly my time is up.

I skip the rest of lunch and head back to the library. The librarian sees it's me and, without a word, comes out with the folder. This time, I read the second newspaper article. It's from July 1921, with the headline "Mysterious Man on Bridge Stalls Train":

Just after midnight, while passing through the town of Middleton, all of the train's passengers were awakened by the train whistle. Engineer James Rook had stopped the train, citing that a man was standing on the railroad bridge. Further investigation found no man on the bridge, in the area, or in the river below.

It sure sounds just like the story of Billy Jones. But is Billy actually doing these things now? It's just too easy to blame it all on a ghost. And a ghost who just gets really mad when people break up? I mean, Dad's ghost isn't going around haunting everyone on Earth that has had an accident on a bridge, right? Besides, I read somewhere that ghosts have to stay in one place. There has to be another explanation.

Again, if I were a detective, I would look at the evidence first—the cold, hard facts—and I would think through all that I know for sure: someone attacked Alex, left a threatening note for Annie in the girl's bathroom, tampered with Kasey's brakes, and planted a messed-up teddy bear on Drew's front steps.

Next I would search for a motive: Why would someone do these things? This is the hardest part for me because I don't know many people in this town yet. It's a stretch, but *Kasey* could have a motive: to prevent Drew from breaking up with her. Maybe she's playing on his superstitions and making it look like Billy Jones is exacting revenge on couples who break up after writing their names on the bridge! But does Kasey really think Drew would stay with her just because of some ghost story?

Wait, I think to myself, *this is crazy. Kasey's your cousin and your best friend—how could you think that she's capable of doing something like this?*

But just as I'm talking myself out of believing it, I remember the red goo that was on the bathroom mirror. Just two days before that, I had seen Kasey bake a cherry pie with my own eyes. She could have snuck into school and used the cherry filling to write on the bathroom mirror. She could have followed Alex that night too. After all, she *did* admit to driving a truck around midnight the night he was run off the road. She also could have left the mangled teddy bear at Drew's house—she has so many that no one would notice if one went missing. She could have even written the note on her own car: in fact, *she* was the one who woke us up to come out and witness it! But the car accident with Isobel and Henry last year? Why would she do something like that?

I refocus my attention to the folder in front of me and find an article about the accident.

"Local Couple in Collision," the headline reads.

Isobel Chen, 17, and Henry Washington, 18, of Middleton, were driving on Old County Road H when Chen lost control of the car. "I saw a guy, he was our age, standing on the bridge," Chen said. "It looked like he was going to jump. I tried to stop the car and it skidded into the wood beam."

Washington also reported seeing the young man. "He was wearing old-timey clothes, a hat, and suspenders," he said. "I told Isobel to pull over, that we had to help. But when we got out of the car, there was no one on the bridge." Emergency personnel were called to the scene, but no one was found. Local meteorologists reported heavy fog in the area.

The warning bell rings, and I nearly jump out of my seat.

I may have gotten more information, but this trip to the library has made me even more concerned than before. *If Kasey's the one behind all of this, who did Isobel and Henry see on the bridge that night?* Not knowing what to do, I decide to go to Mrs. Whyse's office after school. Without giving anything away, maybe she can help me figure out how to approach Kasey.

***

"Is there something you need to talk about, Lucia?" Mrs. Whyse asks when she sees me waiting in her office.

"I'm just worried about everything that's going on," I say. "There have been these

51

strange things happening, you know, with the couples breaking up, Annie and Alex . . ."

"Yes," she says. "Someone is definitely behind these events—the incident with Alex and the truck, the message in the girl's restroom . . . Do you know why someone would do these things?"

"Maybe—I mean—maybe someone's boyfriend is leaving her and if there was a curse, then maybe the boyfriend wouldn't leave. I mean, I would want to go to Mexico too, er, wherever, but maybe she's just really upset because he promised not to leave her, ever," I stammer.

"Yes, people make promises. Sometimes people have to break promises too. You understand that, right?"

"Yes." I nod and look down at my hands.

"The first step is to admit there is a problem," she says.

"Well, there is definitely a prob—"

"The second step is to admit what you did."

Wait, what? "No—I . . . do you think *I* did something?"

"Isn't that what we're talking about here?"

"No! No, Mrs. Whyse, I . . . I'm talking about a friend." I can't help it: my eyes fill with tears. "She made a cherry pie, and she has these teddy bears—"

"Wait, slow down," Mrs. Whyse says, frowning. "What about a teddy bear?"

"My friend left a stabbed teddy bear at her boyfriend's house, and she admitted she was driving his uncle's truck right when Alex said someone tried to run him over."

"Oh boy," Mrs. Whyse says. "Lucia, this is serious. If you have any information about these events, you need to tell me. Who is it that you suspect did these things? Somebody needs to talk to her."

My heart sinks. Kasey is pretty much my best friend, and I don't want to get her into trouble. "Hold on, before I tell you who it is, first let me talk to her and see if she will turn herself in," I plead.

Mrs. Whyse looks unconvinced. "I'm not sure we can wait."

"Please!"

"Okay. But if she won't come in, we may have to get the police involved."

I hope I can talk some sense into Kasey before it's too late.

I barely look at the bridge on the walk home, but the eerie sound of the wind howling under the arches makes my skin crawl. When I get to our front porch steps, I hear voices coming from Patricia and Kasey's kitchen. Thinking it's Kasey, I head over to their front door.

As I step inside, I realize it's Patricia and Tony. They are whispering intently, so I stay hidden in the hallway and listen. Dishes clink, and the fridge opens and shuts. I try to move closer to hear them over the extra noise, but my foot catches on the carpet, and I pitch forward.

"Oh, hi, you guys!" I say too loudly, my face flushing.

"Hi," Patricia says coolly.

"What were you doing there?" Tony stares at me.

"I just got home from school"—I point behind me to the front door—"and I heard a voice and I thought it was Kasey . . . and I want to talk to her."

"Oh," Patricia says and touches Tony's sleeve. "Kasey went over to Drew's for the, um, car thing, but I bet she'll be back in a few minutes." She holds up a pizza box. "Want some mistake pizza?"

We go to the living room, where Patricia and Tony sit in the middle of the couch right next to each other. I want to ask about Kasey's brakes—were they really cut?—but Tony turns on a football game on TV so loud that it's hard to talk.

I take a piece of the cold pizza. It's sausage with extra cheese and green olives and pickled peppers—it really was a mistake. I pick off the olives and peppers and shove half a slice into my mouth.

Patricia mutes the TV when a commercial comes on. "So, how is everything going?" she says.

I cover my mouth and chew the gooey cheese. "Kinda sad, you know, Drew going to Mexico."

Tony nods. "I hope their breakup was worth it," he says. "And that he gets what they promised him out of that exchange program."

"I can't believe he's leaving Kasey all alone," Patricia says.

"Maybe he won't end up leaving her alone," Tony adds darkly. "He might slip up before then. If his grades go down they'll reject him, screw everything up."

"Tony," Patricia says, putting her hand on his arm and giving him a warning look. "Let's not get into all of that."

"Into all of what?" I ask.

"The army!" Tony bursts out angrily. "They told me they'd take me, ROTC. Then I get one, two bad grades and they take back their offer. Bunch of liars!"

Jeez, no wonder he seems so angry all the time. "Were you supposed to maintain a certain grade point average?" I ask, tentatively.

He rolls his eyes, and his face reddens. "They told me I was in! And then they take it away!"

"Tony . . . " Patricia strokes his arm.

Tony shakes off her hand. "People think they can just make a promise and oops!"—he throws his hands up—"change their minds. Well, in this life there are consequences."

"It's okay, T-bear," Patricia says, leaning in close to his face. It looks like this could turn into another epic makeout session, so I get up to leave. Just then Kasey's red car pulls up.

Kasey walks in. She's been crying again.

"Hi!" I say.

"Hey, Lu."

"Have you been crying? What's wrong?" I can't help but ask.

Kasey wipes her cheeks. "It's nothing— I'm fine."

I smile at her. "Okay. Well, um, can I talk to you?"

"Sure."

"In private?" I nod at the lovebirds on the couch.

"Let's go to my room," she says.

We walk to her bedroom, and I pull the door closed and stand with my back to it.

Kasey sits on her bed with her million teddy bears. *Make that a million minus one,* I think.

"Kasey. I know," I say. My heart pounds in my chest.

"You know?" Kasey says. "But how? I haven't told anybody."

"The cherry pie, the teddy bear, Alex's attack, that note on your car. It's not a curse. It's you."

"Lucia? What are you talking about?"

"The bridge. The curse. You have been doing all those things," I say.

Kasey shakes her head. "Um, no, I haven't done anything."

I keep my voice low so Patricia and Tony can't hear. "Kasey, listen to me. I am talking to you first because Mrs. Whyse at school knows something's up, and she's going to go to the police if you don't turn yourself in."

"The police!" Kasey jumps up from the bed. "Are you crazy?"

"I'm not crazy," I say as calmly as I can. She throws her hands up and plops down on the bed so hard that half of the bears bounce up and fall off. I take a large teddy bear and hold it as a shield against . . . I don't know what. But I feel better holding it.

"I want to keep the police out of this," I say. "Kasey, it all points to you. You don't want Drew to break up with you, so you made up this curse and you've been scaring Annie and Alex. You put the red goo on the mirror at school; it was cherry pie filling, wasn't it? I saw you bake that pie. You drove the dark truck that tried to run Alex off the road. You said so yourself—it was Drew's uncle's and you were driving it that night!" I look down at the teddy bear in my hands. "And you stabbed the bear and left it on Drew's doorstep. I don't know if you had anything to do with Isobel and Henry's accident, or why you would do something like that before Drew broke up with you, but if you did it, Kasey, the cops will find out."

She stares at me with big eyes.

"But . . ." Her voice shakes. "There *was* something wrong with my brakes. The mechanic said so. Why would I cut my own brakes?"

I take a breath and say in a very nice, soft voice, "Look at you. You're still crying about him leaving."

"You're wrong, Lucia, about everything. I am sad Drew's going, but I'm going down to visit him in the spring, and he'll be back in May." She gives me a look that I've never seen before.

"No, Kasey, you're way too attached to Drew, and it's making you crazy."

She rises and points her finger in my face. "You're dead wrong. I'm not too attached, but I am attached. Plus, I've been crying out of happiness." She turns her hand and wiggles her ring finger. Circling it is a thin, gold band with the smallest diamond I've ever laid eyes on.

"What is that?" I ask.

"A promise ring."

"A promise to what?"

"A promise to stay together forever."

I drop the teddy bear. Did her plan actually work?

CHAPTER 7

THURSDAY

The next morning is misty, and I try not to look at the bridge as I hurry past it on my way to school. It's not a curse, it's Kasey. Still, something makes me turn my head: a dark figure on the bridge, behind the heavy fog. I turn away. This is what happens when you let your thoughts run amok.

"Did you talk to your friend?" Mrs. Whyse asks when I come into her office.

"Yes," I say. "But she's still not ready to come in. Can you give me until the end of the day? I have one more thing to check."

Mrs. Whyse sighs. "I just don't think that's a good idea. Someone else could get hurt."

"No one will get hurt. My friend doesn't even need the curse anymore—she got what she wanted," I blurt.

"Lucia," Mrs. Whyse says, "an overwrought friend is one thing, but if there's any chance this curse is real, you need to stay away from the bridge."

"But I thought you said—"

"It's for your own good." She raises her eyebrows.

"It's not a curse, though! It's my cousin, Kasey: she's behind all of this, and I can get her to come in."

Mrs. Whyse pauses for a long moment, clearly thinking over what I said. Sighing, she gives in and says, "Okay. Five o'clock. But that's it, no more time."

***

I'm back in the library trying to see if I can find any more information. I've been staring at the articles for a while when the librarian steps out of her office. "Are you okay?" she asks.

"Billy Jones," I say. "You said there wasn't a curse until later. What did you mean?"

"Well . . . all this nonsense about curses didn't really pick up until this year. Sure, some weird things happened, like trains getting stuck and the accident with Henry and Isobel. But nothing like what's been going on this fall—the note in the women's bathroom, Alex's run-in with the black truck, and Mrs. Whyse tells me someone left a stabbed stuffed animal at a student's house! And now"—she shakes her head in disgust—"people really believe there's a curse."

"Both Isobel and Henry said they saw a man on the bridge," I say. "How do you explain that?"

"They were in shock. People in shock imagine things. They knew about the old engineer's story—everyone in town does—and that's what must have come to mind. Henry had whiplash and Isobel had a concussion."

"But—"

She holds up her hands, not in surrender but in protest. "Look, I've lived here all my life," she says. "This is the work of someone who is a little off-kilter and has a bone to pick."

I close my eyes. Does Kasey really have that much of a bone to pick?

"Anything else?" the librarian asks. "We've got some great horror books you could read if you like scary stuff: *Dracula*, *Frankenstein*, even some Stephen King."

I walk to the door and wave. "No, thanks, I've got enough of that in real life."

Somehow it all comes back to the bridge, I think. I feel sick because it's the last place I want to go, but I have to go there in order to figure this out.

I make it through my last three classes and then head out to the bridge. I manage two steps before the planks wobble and I have to grab the iron handrail. It's only ten or so steps to the middle. Even in the fall chill, sweat pours from my face and runs down my neck. I take another tentative step, but the bridge seems to sway and my legs go weak.

I can't do it.

I climb back over the barrier. I head down the grassy embankment, but just like in my dream, a force pushes my feet forward and, just like last time, I'm skidding down the wet hill toward the deep, rushing river. I accidentally slip and slide down the bank into the water. The river gurgles and rushes right below my shoulders, just inches from my head, as I jam my heel against a stone. I'm able to stop and take a long, slow breath. I turn my head slightly, and then I see it.

Far in the corner under the bridge in gold letters, someone has written **Cleo & Mark Antony, one heart, 'til death do us part.**

Cleo. Someone must have finished the paint job that I saw earlier this week. As I pull myself out of the water, I put all my energy into trying to figure out who this Cleo is. Then it hits me: *Cleo, as in Cleopatra . . . it must be Kasey! She has an Egyptian box—Cleopatra must be a weird nickname for her or something.* But I pause mid-thought as I try to fit the rest of the pieces together. Something isn't adding up here— *Who is Mark Antony?*

For the second time in a week, I get home soaking wet. Kasey looks up from her book when I get to the porch.

She barely nods. "Still think I'm out to get people?" she asks.

"Cleo?" I ask.

She gives me a confused look. "Who?"

"The box," I say. "With the Egyptian stuff on it. Cleopatra, that's your nickname, right?

"Mine? No, that's Patricia. Apparently Tony calls her Cleo, as in Cleo-Patricia, so he got her that Egyptian-themed box or something." She rolls her eyes. "Corny, right?"

One heart, 'til death do us part. "So Cleopatra and Mark Antony . . . are Patricia and Tony?"

She shrugs and gets up to walk back into the duplex. "I guess. Like I said, pretty corny. I have to get go—"

"Wait! One question—didn't you tell me Patricia got kicked out of her house?"

"Yeah," she says. "Her mom didn't like Tony, but Patricia promised Tony she wouldn't break up with him. Something happened, but I don't know what. Anyway, she got thrown out because of it."

Patricia promised Tony. I saw how angry he got when he was thinking about the military breaking their promise to him. And his heated reaction to Kasey and Drew's breakup definitely seemed a bit strange. Apparently he has a problem with other people breaking their promises too . . .

Suddenly—finally—everything starts to make sense. It's not a curse . . . but maybe it's not Kasey either. *Maybe Tony is the one behind these attacks!* I already know that Patricia didn't do anything—at least there was no way that she could have damaged Kasey's brakes or brought the teddy bear to Drew's house. Besides, she's so enamored with Tony that she probably can't even see how crazy he can be. But before I say anything, I have to be sure it's really him.

CHAPTER 8

THURSDAY NIGHT

Mom beeps at me as she pulls into the
driveway. She gets out, and I can tell right away
she's tired because her hair is totally flat and
her makeup is smudged under her eyes. Mom,
raccoon flight attendant, home at last.

"Hi, Mom!" I call and give her a hug. I
am glad she's home, but I'm not sure how I'll
explain all that's happened.

"Did you have a good trip?" I ask as I
follow her back into the house. I sit down at the
table while she puts the teakettle on.

"Yeah. I guess. We hit a storm so I didn't
sleep much. Had some great sushi, though.

Oh! And I got you this." She pulls out a bunch of Japanese candy and a necklace. *Why would I need a necklace? She knows I don't take off the eagle pendant, doesn't she?* It was in Dad's hands, on his key ring, when they found him. The truck must have stalled on the bridge, and he tried to start it.

I rub the pendant between my fingers. I like to think it keeps part of his spirit always near my heart. Maybe this is Mom's way of trying to help me move on? "Thanks," I force myself to say.

"So, anything interesting happen around here?" Mom asks.

Um . . . "Not much." I look at the clock and swallow the lump in my throat. Mrs. Whyse said I had until 5:00 today, and it's already 4:30. "Except . . ." I start, then swallow again. "Except someone is harassing couples who break up, but only if they've written their names on the bridge, promising to stay together."

"Woah, what? Harassing?" She drops two tea bags into two cups. "How?"

"Well, driving too close behind them at night, writing in red *something* on the wall in one of the girls' bathrooms, mangling teddy bears . . ."

"How do you mangle a teddy bear?"

"Well, you stab it and tear out its eyes."

"Oh my," she says just as the teakettle whistles. She pours steaming water into the cups, and the aromas of ginger and cloves fill the air. "Who's doing all these terrible things?"

I take my cup and inhale, deciding on how to explain my suspicions, just as a car pulls up out front. I go to the door. "Mrs. Whyse, my counselor from school, is here to talk about it. We will fill you in."

***

"So, Lucia," Mrs. Whyse says as we meet her on the front porch, "is Kasey ready to turn herself in?" She raises her eyebrows at us and crosses her arms.

Mom looks at me with surprised eyes. "Kasey?" she gasps.

"Mrs. Whyse, I figured out that it's not Kasey. I think Tony's behind it."

"Tony? Patricia's boyfriend?" Mom says.

I nod. "He's the only one who seems angry enough about all the breakups to do these things.

Mom sips her tea. "I'm just glad it's not Kasey. So, what do we do now?"

"I think we talk to Patricia," Mrs. Whyse says.

***

"What's up, kid?" Patricia says as she comes into our living room. Her face drops when she sees that Mom and Mrs. Whyse are here too.

"Do you want to tell us about you and Tony, or should I say Cleo and Mark Antony?"

Patricia looks like she just ate a bug. "What about us? That we wrote our names on the bridge? Big deal."

"That's maybe all you did. But not Tony. He's behind the 'curse.' He attacked Henry last year and probably caused their accident. He wrote *LIAR* in red goo on the bathroom wall, followed Alex in the truck, stabbed the teddy bear, messed with Kasey's brakes, and wrote the note Kasey found on her car."

She swallows and drops onto the couch. "What are you talking about? It couldn't have been him." She blinks slowly, her face losing all color.

"Why not?" I sit right next to her.

"Good question," Mrs. Whyse says.

Patricia turns to Mom and Mrs. Whyse and says, "Because I was with Tony when all of that happened." She pulls out her red sparkly phone. "I'll show you." I watch as she types in her password, five-six-eight-three, chanting "L-O-V-E" under her breath. *Ew.*

"Where was Tony the night Alex was almost run off the road?" I ask.

Patricia shifts on the couch. "He'd called in sick to work, so I went to his house to bring him soup." She holds her phone up and shows a picture of her and Tony on the couch, eating soup. "I took this that night."

"That only takes a few minutes," I say. "He could have left later."

"No," Patricia says, "because I stayed with him for the rest of the night watching movies and I didn't leave until past midnight. So it couldn't have been him."

"You're sure of this?" Mrs. Whyse says.

Patricia stands up. "Yes. And I will testify in court that it wasn't him." She storms out the door.

Mrs. Whyse clasps her hands together and says, "Good—she may have to."

CHAPTER 9

SATURDAY

My cell phone rings at eight in the morning.
Who calls at eight on a Saturday? It's Mrs.
Whyse, who says she's coming over to talk to
Patricia again. I think about going back to sleep,
but I just had that cliff dream again and almost
fell right out of bed. I can hardly believe the
events of yesterday. It has to be Tony. He even
said when he got angry about the army rescinding
his ROTC scholarship that people who break
their promises should suffer the consequences.

Just after nine Mrs. Whyse pulls up. Mom
is sound asleep and snoring, so I close the door
to her room. I can handle this myself.

Mrs. Whyse and I walk to Patricia's side of the duplex. Patricia meets us at the door wearing a pair of sweats and a pink hoodie—the same clothes she wore yesterday.

"Can we talk to you for a moment?" Mrs. Whyse says.

Patricia shrugs and steps out onto the porch.

Mrs. Whyse says, "You swear you were with Tony the whole time the night the truck tried to run Alex off the road?"

Patricia's hair is mussed and dark circles show under her eyes. She casually leans in the doorway, a hint of a sneer appearing on her face. "Well, no. I wasn't there the whole time."

"I knew it!" I blurt.

Mrs. Whyse shoots me a look, and I cover my mouth with my hand.

"He left in his truck, was gone for about an hour, and then came back," Patricia says.

"What was he wearing?" Mrs. Whyse asks.

Patricia confidently puts one hand on her hip. "Jeans and a black hoodie."

"All black?" Mrs. Whyse asks.

"Yeah," Patricia says. "Except for a skull and crossbones on the back."

"I'm going to the police," Mrs. Whyse says.

Just then, Tony's truck roars up the driveway.

"Oh no," I say. "We have to get out of here."

Patricia, straightens up, smirks, and crosses her arms over her chest. "That's a great idea," she says, rolling her eyes. "Maybe I have to get out of here too."

Mrs. Whyse tries to talk some sense into her: "Patricia, you might not be safe yourself." We hear Tony's door slam. "You need to stay away from him!"

I look to see Tony leaning against his truck, the engine still running. He has his arms crossed and a cruel grin on his face.

"Well, well," he says, "looks like a party. Unfortunately, we're just leaving." He nods his head in the direction of Patricia, and I see she's hastily throwing clothes in a suitcase.

"You don't have to do this," Mrs. Whyse tries to reason with her. "We can keep you safe, I promise."

"Yeah right," Patricia laughs. "Just like my parents, you can't see the truth. Don't you get it? I'll always be safe with Tony." She hustles past us, dragging her suitcase behind her. Tony gets in the driver's side and puts the truck in reverse. Just as Patricia opens the passenger side door, she stops and turns to us.

"Tony gets it," she says. "You can't count on anyone. They'll break their promises and let you down every time. So we're counting on each other." She gets in the truck, and Tony peels out of the driveway.

I walk down the driveway, dust swirling around me. The day looks just like it did in my dream—dark and foggy. After a few minutes I find myself walking the path to the bridge.

CHAPTER 10

MONDAY

It's actually not raining today. I even see a
patch of blue sky on the far edge, but you can
never be sure here how long a clear day
will last.

At least I now know who was behind it
all. Not Kasey, not a ghost, not Patricia,
but Tony. Maybe some time and distance
from Middleton will help soften Tony and
Patricia's anger. After she left, I woke Kasey
up and told her I was wrong. She was upset,
but she told me she'd get over it by the time
we started our coffee shop. Mom called
the police when she woke up and I told her

Patricia was gone, but no one has any idea where she and Tony went. I told the police how Patricia admitted that it was Tony who had been doing everything, and the police promised that they would keep an eye out for them. At least we don't have to worry about haunted bridges anymore.

It's too early to show up at school. Instead, I walk to the barrier and swing my leg over.

The sun finds a hole in the overcast sky and beams down on the bridge. It doesn't look scary now, just old and sad.

There is no ghost. Just some names written on a bridge—names that will always stay, unlike people. I take a step forward, then another. Near the middle of the bridge, I peer out at the mist on the green water.

Patricia and Tony are gone. Dad is gone.
But Kasey's still here. And Mom and
Aunt Jane.

My eyes fill with tears. "I miss you, Dad," I say out over the river. I let go of the iron beam and walk the last few steps to the other side—I made it.

I touch my eagle pendant, knowing Dad would be proud of me for conquering my fears.

A bank of clouds moves in, and the sun is gone. As I walk back across the bridge, stepping carefully over the gaps, I get the feeling I am being watched, but as I scan the area I see no one.

I reach the barrier and swing my legs over. It feels good. If I got through that, I can get through anything. Patricia and Tony may have disappeared without owning up to what they did, but things will be okay. We—Kasey, Mom, Aunt Jane, me—will be okay.

ABOUT THE AUTHOR

J. Fallenstein likes to freak herself out by constantly asking "what if?" She writes sometimes-scary stories that answer that question. You can find her at midnight in the Midwest wide awake wondering what that noise was.